MR.BRAVE

MR.BRAVE

by Roger Hargreaves

Mr Brave is not as strong
as Mr Strong.

He is not as tall as Mr Tall.

But that does not stop him being brave,
as you will soon see.

Now, last Tuesday, Little Miss Bossy invited
Mr Brave to tea.

"AND DON'T BE LATE!" she shouted
down the phone.

It was a very stormy day, but Mr Brave
knew that Little Miss Bossy's temper was worse.

So he set off for Little Miss Bossy's house,
hurrying along as fast as he could
to be sure that he was not late for tea.

Along the way he heard a cry for help.

It was Mr Messy.

He had been blown into the river by the wind.

Mr Brave did not want to be late for Little Miss Bossy
but, being the brave fellow he was,
he jumped in and rescued Mr Messy.

Wet right through,
he hurried along the lane.

Suddenly, he heard someone sobbing loudly.

Who could it be?

It was Little Miss Somersault!

She was balancing on a tightrope
tied between two tall trees!

"Oh, Mr Brave, I'm so lonely," she sobbed.
"Nobody will come and play on my tightrope!
They are all too frightened of heights.
You're so brave, won't you come
and join me?"

Mr Brave looked up at Little Miss Somersault.

Then he thought about Little Miss Bossy,
but, being the brave fellow he was,
he took pity on Little Miss Somersault
and climbed up on to the tightrope.

They chatted away happily for a while
until Mr Brave happened to look down.

"Little Miss Somersault! Look!
The rope is going to snap!
We're going to fall ...
and it's such a long way to the bottom.
Oh, calamity! Oh, help!" he cried out in panic.

"Be brave, Mr Brave," said Little Miss Somersault.

And without more ado,
she carried him safely back
down to the ground.

"Oh, thank you," said Mr Brave,
with a sigh of relief.

Little Miss Somersault said goodbye.

And Mr Brave was left on his own,
shaking like a leaf.

"I don't deserve to be called Mr Brave,
I was scared stiff! Thank goodness
nobody knows my secret,"
he said to himself.

And nobody does know his secret,
or do they?

Little Miss Trouble just happened to be passing and had seen everything.

And what she had seen and heard had given her an idea.

A very naughty idea!

She grinned a mischievous grin.

"Hey, come here everybody, come and see this!" she shouted at the top of her voice.

Very quickly a large crowd gathered.

"I have an announcement,"
announced Little Miss Trouble.
"Did you know that Mr Brave isn't brave at all?"

"No, it can't be true," said the crowd, all together.

"It is true!" said Little Miss Trouble,
"and I'll prove it to you."

"Mr Brave," she continued,
"I dare you to walk across that tightrope!"

Mr Brave looked up at the tightrope.

And all the crowd looked up at the tightrope.

Then all the crowd looked at Mr Brave.

Mr Brave suddenly remembered something.

A very important something.

"Just look at the time!" he cried.
"I'm going to be late
for tea at Little Miss Bossy's!"

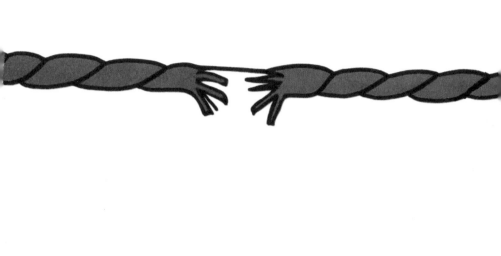

"Must dash!" he cried.

And he ran off as quickly as possible.

"Hooray!" cheered the crowd.

And they all clapped and applauded Mr Brave.

Little Miss Trouble looked puzzled.

"Why are you all cheering him?" she cried.
"He ran away! He isn't brave at all!"

"Oh, yes he is!" they all shouted.
"Would you turn up late for tea at
Little Miss Bossy's house?"

Little Miss Trouble thought for a moment.
"Gosh, he is brave after all!" she said in awe.

3 Great Offers for MR.MEN Fans!

MR. MEN TOKEN

1 New Mr. Men or Little Miss Library Bus Presentation Cases

A brand new stronger, roomier school bus library box, with sturdy carrying handle and stay-closed fasteners.

The full colour, wipe-clean boxes make a great home for your full collection.

They're just £5.99 inc P&P and free bookmark!

☐ MR. MEN ☐ LITTLE MISS (please tick and order overleaf)

2 Door Hangers and Posters

In every Mr. Men and Little Miss book like this one, you will find a special token. Collect 6 tokens and we will send you a brilliant Mr. Men or Little Miss poster and a Mr. Men or Little Miss double sided full colour bedroom door hanger of your choice. Simply tick your choice in the list and tape a 50p coin for your two items to this page.

PLEASE STICK YOUR 50P COIN HERE

Door Hangers (please tick)
☐ Mr. Nosey & Mr. Muddle
☐ Mr. Slow & Mr. Busy
☐ Mr. Messy & Mr. Quiet
☐ Mr. Perfect & Mr. Forgetful
☐ Little Miss Fun & Little Miss Late
☐ Little Miss Helpful & Little Miss Tidy
☐ Little Miss Busy & Little Miss Brainy
☐ Little Miss Star & Little Miss Fun

Posters (please tick)
☐ MR.MEN
☐ LITTLE MISS

3 Sixteen Beautiful Fridge Magnets – any 2 for £2.00! inc.P&P

They're very special collector's items!
Simply tick your first and second* choices from the list below of any 2 characters!

1st Choice
- ☐ Mr. Happy
- ☐ Mr. Lazy
- ☐ Mr. Topsy-Turvy
- ☐ Mr. Bounce
- ☐ Mr. Bump
- ☐ Mr. Small
- ☐ Mr. Snow
- ☐ Mr. Wrong

- ☐ Mr. Daydream
- ☐ Mr. Tickle
- ☐ Mr. Greedy
- ☐ Mr. Funny
- ☐ Little Miss Giggles
- ☐ Little Miss Splendid
- ☐ Little Miss Naughty
- ☐ Little Miss Sunshine

2nd Choice
- ☐ Mr. Happy
- ☐ Mr. Lazy
- ☐ Mr. Topsy-Turvy
- ☐ Mr. Bounce
- ☐ Mr. Bump
- ☐ Mr. Small
- ☐ Mr. Snow
- ☐ Mr. Wrong

- ☐ Mr. Daydream
- ☐ Mr. Tickle
- ☐ Mr. Greedy
- ☐ Mr. Funny
- ☐ Little Miss Giggles
- ☐ Little Miss Splendid
- ☐ Little Miss Naughty
- ☐ Little Miss Sunshine

*Only in case your first choice is out of stock.

TO BE COMPLETED BY AN ADULT

To apply for any of these great offers, ask an adult to complete the coupon below and send it with the appropriate payment and tokens, if needed, to MR. MEN CLASSIC OFFER, PO BOX 715, HORSHAM RH12 5WG

☐ Please send ____ Mr. Men Library case(s) and/or ____ Little Miss Library case(s) at £5.99 each inc P&P

☐ Please send a poster and door hanger as selected overleaf. I enclose six tokens plus a 50p coin for P&P

☐ Please send me ____ pair(s) of Mr. Men/Little Miss fridge magnets, as selected above at £2.00 inc P&P

Fan's Name _____

Address _____

_____ **Postcode** _____

Date of Birth _____

Name of Parent/Guardian _____

Total amount enclosed £ _____

☐ **I enclose a cheque/postal order payable to Egmont Books Limited**

☐ **Please charge my MasterCard/Visa/Amex/Switch or Delta account** (delete as appropriate)

Card Number

Expiry date ___/___ **Signature** _____

MR.MEN   LITTLE MISS
Mr. Men and Little Miss™ & ©Mrs. Roger Hargreaves

CUT ALONG DOTTED LINE AND RETURN THIS WHOLE PAGE